ACCUSED!

A story of Beatrix Laing

by

Susan Greig

rooshie doo

Published by Gallus Publications,
PO Box 29055,
Dunfermline KY11 4YL

Cover design by Liam Doherty, with original artwork by Jenna Rankin (front cover) and Leighann Russell (back cover), both of Commercial Primary School, Dunfermline. Illustrations by Frank McCormick.

ISBN 0-9546625-4-7

A catalogue record for this book is available from the British Library.

Printed and bound by Printing Services (Scotland) Ltd., Broomhead Drive, Dunfermline.

Author's acknowledgements

Much of the historical background for this book comes from the
writings of Stuart MacDonald and the late Christine Larner, of
Knox College, Toronto. I owe them my thanks.

Susan Greig
London, Ontario
June 2004

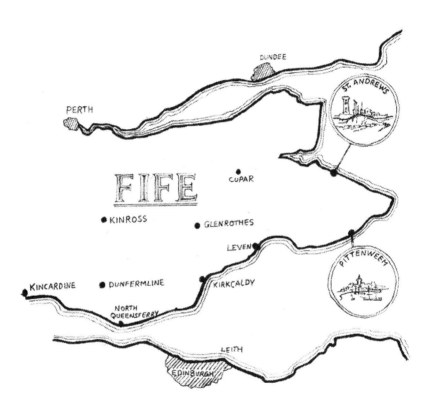

PERTH

DUNDEE

ST. ANDREWS

FIFE

CUPAR

KINROSS

GLENROTHES

LEVEN

PITTENWEEM

KINCARDINE

DUNFERMLINE

KIRKCALDY

NORTH
QUEENSFERRY

LEITH

EDINBURGH

CHAPTER ONE

Seven times eight is … fifty six. There! My last problem for today!

Mr Laidlaw has charged me with continuing my schoolwork while he is gone on his business to Edinburgh - four whole days - how I wish it was not so long! I still get scared if he is away and hate it when he leaves us. I know I will not be happy and content again until his return.

So, while Mr Laidlaw is away, I am to continue teaching Davey his numbers and letters (he can already count to 100 and write both his name and mine). We are going to practise writing Mr Laidlaw's name, which is William, as a great surprise for him. He gave me a special gift before he left - my very own book, a journal, in which I am to write of all the things that happened to Davey and me in Fife last year. It has a braw blue cover, the colour of the sky in summer, and Miss Laidlaw has written my name on it on the front, in her very best handwriting. And no one is to write anything in it but me. Mr Laidlaw says that it is very important that someone who was there should tell the truth about what happened in Fife. Maybe then, he says, such terrible things will never happen again in Scotland.

Now I have finished my schoolwork, I'm going to start my journal in my special place, sitting in my favourite tree in the garden. Of course, I am much braver than Davey who is only six after all. *I* can climb nigh to the top of the tree, so that when I stretch my fingers out as far as they can go, peeping up right through the branches, I almost touch the sky. I can hear people and watch them, but I am invisible - and that makes me feel very safe indeed.

Miss Laidlaw, knowing that I want to write in my journal, has taken Davey for a walk. Miss Laidlaw keeps house for us all and looks after Davey and me. She can be very stern and strict and it is ever so easy to make her crabbit. Once, Davey and I ate every last apple out of the bowl in the kitchen. Davey ate six apples, and he was very sick to the stomach. I ate seven, and wasn't sick at all, but Miss Laidlaw was *just* as crabbit with me as with Davey! Sometimes I wish I was the younger sister. Then Davey would have to be in charge of making our bed and doing our chores and being responsible.

Being responsible is one of those things I have learnt a great deal about since coming to live here, indeed Miss Laidlaw speaks of it constantly. Mr Laidlaw says the people in Fife were not responsible for what they did to Aunt Bee or Janet Cornfoot. They were like the crowds who killed our Lord, he says, 'they knew not what they did'.

Miss Laidlaw says Davey and I have brought much added responsibility to her and I think this must be a heavy burden to her and is why she is so stern and strict. Yet I know she likes us, even so. One night, not long after our arrival, I sat and listened to her talking to Mr Laidlaw in the candlelight when they both thought I was fast asleep.

'Really William, you have no further responsibility to those children. You feed them, clothe them and educate them.'

'And pray tell me Maggie, if I had left them in Pittenweem, what would have become of them?'

'Oh someone would have taken them in, neighbours, a local family, that old man who was caring for them.'

'Maggie, you were not there. The fear and anger in the town were very high at the time - God have mercy on that poor woman that was lynched. If I had not offered to take the children they would still be at terrible risk... I could not leave them Maggie, I could not. Besides' (and I fancied I heard a smile in his voice), 'are they so much trouble to us? Do they not lighten up our tired old lives with their smiles and games and hugs?'

'They are affectionate children, I grant you and biddable enough I suppose. Still, it is a lot of extra work looking after them, William.'

'And am I not grateful everyday for all you do? Do I not thank God every day for your care for the wee souls, for agreeing to take them in when no one else would? Am I not blessed with having a true Christian woman for a sister?'

Miss Laidlaw's voice also had a smile in it: 'William Laidlaw, you are a blether of the first order and why I listen to you and put up with your havering, I don't know. You could charm the birds off the trees.'

'Nay lass, that would be God's work, not mine.'

And I could hear them both laughing gently together as I hugged myself happily and fell at last to sleep.

CHAPTER TWO:

Mr Laidlaw said I should begin my journal by telling all about who I am. My name is Isobel Meldrum and I am almost ten years old. But my wee brother Davey calls me Iso. I am very tall for my age, with a freckled nose and fair hair that falls around my face, no matter how I comb it back. Combing my hair and keeping it tidy is one of my main responsibilities and a real scunner it is, let me tell you! There is no doubt that my hair is a sore trial to Miss Laidlaw.

I can count to 1,000 and have read all the Psalms in the Bible. Mr Laidlaw says the Psalms are a good place to start with the Bible. My favourite is the nineteenth Psalm: 'The heavens declare the glory of God, the skies proclaim the work of his hands.' It was my Mother's favourite. Sometimes, when I read it, I can still hear her voice in my head, reading it along with me.

Davey cannot read the Psalms yet but then he can hardly read at all. He is still only a baby really. We do play together though and we sleep together in our own wee room right at the very top of the house, where it is very quiet and safe. We were to have a bed each, but Davey still gets nightmares, so he likes to sleep in bed close by me. When I am 10, Miss Laidlaw is going to allow me to have a candle in our room, that I will be able to light it when Davey or I wake from a nightmare. She is always the one who comes to us in the night, and she is never stern nor cross with us then, but holds us very tight and whispers over and over again: 'Wheest my bonnie bairns, wheest. You are safe and you are loved, wheest. No harm will befall you here. Wheest.' And she kisses our hair and strokes our faces so gently, never leaving us until we are asleep.

Davey and I live with the Laidlaws because there is no one else to look after us. My father died a long time ago and I do not remember him so well. He was a fisherman but one day there was a terrible accident on the boat and he was killed and Mother was left to bring us up all by herself.

Then one day Mother herself became sick. She could no longer work and we lost our house because we could not pay the rent. It was then that we moved in with Aunt Beatrix, her elder sister. I am not sure that Aunt Bee really wanted us to come, but she could see that Mother could no longer care for us herself.

When she got a little stronger, Mother took over the kitchen and the garden, to help Aunt Bee. She grew lots of our food. Davey and I loved to help in the garden. Davey's job was clearing out all the stones and pebbles and putting them in a big heap at the side. Mine was to clear the weeds and thistles and to sow the seeds and plants in very straight rows. Mother grew all sorts of herbs, and she and Aunt Bee would use these to help us when we were sick with a fever or a tummy ache. Both Mother and Aunt Bee were marvellously gifted with plants and herbs.

Although she was sad about my Father, Mother loved me and Davey very much. She used to tell us stories about the times before Davey and I were born - we would

cuddle up to her, safe and snug together. Aunt Bee would watch the three of us and sometimes tell us things that we had not heard before about Mother when she was a little girl. The four of us, Mother, Aunt Bee, Davey and I lived very quietly in our village doing no harm to anybody, after Father's death.

But Mother became sick again and this time grew weaker and weaker. Mostly, she would lie quietly in Aunt Bee's bed, hardly moving. One morning, when we kissed her goodbye before heading out for the day, she could not even open her eyes to smile at us, as she usually did. Davey and I spent a busy, happy day down at the harbour and were rewarded for our labours by one of the captains, with four shining silver fish to take home and have for our supper. I can still recall the smell of those fish and feel the weight of them dangling from my fingers as we saw Aunt Bee come out of the cottage to meet us. I knew before she spoke, what she had come to tell us: Mother had died, just minutes before.

The funeral was very hard for us although everyone was very kind and   spoke of Mother being at peace at last and in heaven with Father and our Lord. I know this is so, but I know Davey and I would give anything to have her back with us in *this* world again.

CHAPTER THREE

Aunt Bee's cottage was on the edge of the village on a hill, shaded all round by trees. She helped with the delivery of babies for all the village families. Mother said Aunt Bee was very gifted with young mothers and babies and keeping them safe. Yet, as a widow, with no children of her own, Aunt Bee's ways were a little rough and ready. At least that is what Mother used to say. Aunt Bee was very used to having to please no one but herself. It was hard for her to change after all those years on her own, and we lived together uneasily for many months after Mother's death.

Now and again, Aunt Bee's temper would flare up. On the morning it all started, there was a terrible uproar in our cottage.

Davey, the eejit, had gone outside and brought in a wee dead mouse that a cat had left on our path. The wee thing was all mockit from the overnight storm. Davey was waving the poor wee beastie around by the tail, spinning it faster and faster. When Aunt Bee realized what he was doing, she let out a fierce cry: 'Davey!'. Well, her roar gave him such a fright he leapt right up in the air and let go of the mouse. It soared through the air and landed 'plop' on top of his porridge plate. There it lay, the poor wee thing, one eye staring up at the ceiling, t'other down into the porridge. Aunt Bee did not take it well:

'Davey Meldrum, ye're a prize eejit, bringin' thon filthy mockit critter in ma house! Come here till I get a hold o ye.'

And she chased him round and round the table, till finally she caught up with him and gave him a right stoat on the lug.

Poor Davey sat snivelling in the corner and rocking on his stool. Truth be told, I did feel a wee bit sorry for him. But then what happened but the eejit fell off his stool! He made to run away from Aunt Bee as she lunged at him and toppled backwards, and the leg fell off the stool. I don't know when I have ever seen Aunt Bee so mad.

She stormed over and picked up the leg of the stool, trying to put it together again and muttering away to herself.

'Iso, I'll need to see Morton about some nails for this. Bide here and make sure *he* does no more damage. And tidy up this midden while I'm gone, understand?'

She glared at us, grabbed her shawl from off the

hook by the door and bustled off down the path fuming in a cloud of rage and fury. It was a miserable dreich day out. Aunt Bee told me later that she stepped in one of the storm puddles right up to her knees as she made her way along to the Smiddy.

So, you can see that by the time Aunt Bee reached Morton's Smiddy to collect some nails to repair our stool, she was just 'rarin' for a fight' as she later told me. Patrick, the blacksmith's son, was not able to get the nails ready just then and she gave him a fair tongue lashing, just as she had our Davey. Mind you, she told us later that he was just as rude to her as she was to him, and as crabbit. But he would not budge and get her the nails she needed, so she left him in a right fankle, muttering away to herself.

Maybe I should tell you a little about Patrick Morton. I don't really know him that well - I'm just a bairn as far as he is concerned and Davey even more so. He has no time for bairns like us and if he notices us at all, it is just to tease or name call. Patrick would hang around the harbour and that is where we would usually see him. Once, it was Patrick who hauled Davey out of the harbour with a boathook. Of course, practically every summer one bairn or another ends up in the harbour from tripping over one thing or backing into another. Someone always fished them out. This time though Patrick Morton was the nearest and he grabbed the hook and hauled Davey out of the water – poor Davey looking like a wee drowned rat. So, we had every reason to be grateful to Patrick, which makes what happened next all the harder to understand.

Patrick became ill - very ill indeed. It happened suddenly, after the fight with Aunt Bee. He said that the day after their fight he passed our house and saw her 'mouthing spells and charms' and 'acursing him'. There is no doubt he did get sick. Mr. Cowper, the Minister, went to visit with him many times because of it. Now, Mr. Cowper is very responsible about witchcraft. He preaches to us about how we should be alert and on our guard against such things. He warns us constantly about the reality of witchcraft and how we must protect against it because it could come between us and God. Mr. Cowper began to listen to Patrick and to what he was saying about Aunt Bee and their fight. Folk began to avoid Aunt Bee, and not just Aunt Bee, but Davey and myself too.

Whispers and rumours started to spread right round our village. Folk would not meet our eyes. We began to notice them avoiding us in the braes and lanes. At first,

Aunt Bee just shrugged things off, saying that no one would believe 'thon great lummox' Patrick. But when she heard that Mr. Cowper had been visiting and that he seemed to believe Patrick's accusations, she did begin to worry. One night Old Tom came to tell us that Patrick had accused Aunt Bee of being a witch, in front of Mr. Cowper and some others, and what's more, said Tom, Mr. Cowper believed him and was sending someone from the Kirk Session to command Aunt Bee to appear before them.

It was Mr. Bruce and Mr. Kincaid, two of the Kirk Elders, who came to see Aunt Bee. They would not come into the house, but stood huddled together on the path, seven or eight paces from the door. They had come to tell Aunt Bee of the accusations made by Patrick Morton against her, 'that being witchcraft, charming and malefice'. I can still remember how these great big brave men would not look directly at Aunt Bee, how they shuffled from one foot to the other, and seemed to be on the point of scurrying down our path even before they could get their words out.

Aunt Bee stood as still as a rock and listened to everything they had to say. Only when they finished, did she speak:

'Sirs, I am no witch. A lie may damn my soul to hell, and I tell you, I am no witch'

Mr. Bruce (whose baby Aunt Bee had delivered, only the month before) did look a little ashamed when she said this, but repeated that Aunt Bee must attend the Session to answer the charges.

And that was the beginning. Davey and I had lost our Father, our Mother and now we were about to lose Aunt Bee.

CHAPTER FOUR

Although I love living with the Laidlaws, I do miss the sea. My village of Pittenweem is surrounded by the sea and every day the sea is different: some days blue, some days green and on stormy days, inky black and angry. Mother used to say that the sea paints us a fresh new picture every day and Aunt Bee used to hush her for being fanciful. But I loved her idea of a new picture every day.

Aunt Bee remembers when our harbour was badly neglected and hardly any boats would come in, but Davey and I have only ever known it as the most exciting place in the world. Tall ships arrive from Europe, bringing rich smelling barrels of wine, delicate little potteries, pantiles, bales of cloth and all manner of things. Dozens of people bustle around, dashing here and there, calling out in English and Scots, in French and Dutch, helping to offload the cargoes and then reloading the boats with salt and coal from Fife, to take back across the water.

Growing up, we would hear stories from everyone about amazing and terrible things that can happen at sea. Folk know that the fairies and sea dwellers can cause a storm to blow up or a ship to sink, in the flash of an eye. To ensure good fortune when a ship is about to sail, the women bide indoors. So too the minister - the men will not sail even if they catch just the teeniest glimpse of the minister on their walk to the harbour. Ministers are *never, ever* allowed on a boat. Mother told us of a time when the boats did not sail because Old Tom accidentally came across the minister on his walk to the harbour. Tom told everyone and so the boats stayed safely moored that day. That very night the most dreadful storm arose - everyone would surely have been drowned had they sailed.

Pigs escaping is another terrible warning. On the day that Aunt Bee was brought before the Kirk Session, some pigs escaped and ran pell mell all the way to the harbour. For weeks now, Davey and I had been living in great fear of what would happen if Patrick were believed - those escaped pigs were the worst possible sign of what lay ahead.

Afore she left for the session, Aunt Bee gave us both a rough kiss and told us that she would be 'back afore ye know it'. If by any chance she did not come back that night, we were to find Old Tom, who had been a good friend of our Father. She said that she had spoken with him and he would know what to do.

'But hae nae mind of that, our Isobel. I will be back.'
She bustled about gathering her shawl and fiddling with
some plates and bowls on the table. Her eyes darted
anxiously from Davey to me and back again.

'But mind you look after Davey for me?'

'Of course Aunt Bee, of course I will.'

'Fine then. I'll be off, lass.' With one last look around
our wee cottage she marched out the door.

Davey and I sat with our bowl of oatmeal and half heartedly finished our meal. Our cottage had just the one room and very little furniture - two chairs, two stools, a table and a bed in the corner for Aunt Bee. Davey and I slept on small mattresses in one corner. Our few pots and pans hung on nails driven into the wall, as did our few clothes. The main source of heat and light was our fire, but this was low and smoky that day, and I had to work hard to keep it from
going out. After a while, Davey curled up in the corner and fell asleep, but I was restless and just wandered around, lifting this and straightening that, just like Aunt Bee had done before she left.

Now the Kirk Session was certainly not a place for children, yet I longed to know what was happening with Aunt Bee. I could not settle to anything. If only there was some way I could sneak in and hear what was going on. But there was nowhere to hide in the Kirk, and I was sure to be caught and no doubt punished severely. The Kirk had a broken window damaged in a bad storm only the week before, that had not yet been repaired. It would be ideal for me to 'spy' from, but it was much too high to reach, so I abandoned that idea and sat listening to the rain drip, drip, dripping on the leaves of the trees outside our cottage. I watched a small bird hop steadily from branch to branch climbing up a tree and realized there *was* a way. The great oak tree at the church stood almost next to that broken window. If I climbed just halfway up and crawled right to the end of a branch, I would be able to see in and maybe even hear all that was happening. After all, I was the best climber in the village by far. But if I was caught? I didn't dare think what would happen to me.

'Well, I thought to myself' as a cold shiver ran down my back, 'Better just make sure I don't get caught!'

CHAPTER FIVE

I hunkered down close by my brother and gave him a wee
prod.

'Davey, Davey.'

He rolled over from where he was still dozing in
the shadows and slowly opened his eyes.

'Iso - what is it?'

'Davey, I am going along to see what I can find out.'

'Iso, no!' he cried, at once wide awake. 'If they catch you, they will do something terrible to you. Don't go, don't go!' he pleaded.

'No, wheest, they'll niver catch me, Davey. Listen to me. I am going to climb the big oak tree, you know the one?'

He nodded, 'Aye.'

'See, I will climb richt up, quiet as a wee mouse and I'll peep in thon broken windae, and listen. I will find out all that I can and come straight back here.' I gave him a hug, 'I promise, I will come straight back here.'

'But what if Aunt Bee comes back and finds you gone? What do I tell her?' asked Davey, catching my hand.

My heart sank as I realized that Davey still thought that Aunt Bee would be back to bide with us that night.

'Why then Davey, you can tell her where I'm gone and that I'll be richt back. See?' I gave him my biggest smile.

'Promise, Iso?'

'Promise, Davey.'

I left him sitting on his wee bed in the corner, waving at me as I walked down the path. Pulling Aunt Bee's old shawl over my head and shoulders I walked as quickly and quietly as I could, taking the back braes along to the Kirk. Keeping in the shadows, I dashed over to the oak tree and scrambled up the first few branches, until I was high enough to peep in through the broken window. It took my eyes a few moments to adjust to the inside of the Kirk, which was full of mist and shadows.

I could see that there were perhaps seven or eight

people gathered in the darkness. Mr. Cowper the Minister of course, and also Mr. Kincaid and Mr. Bruce who had come to our house that day. I also saw a couple of the bailies and some others. Aunt Bee sat on a stool before them all. Mr. Cowper was speaking to her:

'Beatrix Laing, in summary, you are by habit and repute a witch, feared as such in this community.'

Aunt Bee glared back at the Minister and repeated what she had said to Mr. Bruce and Mr. Kincaid:

'Sirs, a lie may damn my soul to hell. I am clear of the witchcraft for which I am presently to suffer.'

Mr. Cowper grunted and waved this assertion aside. 'Beatrix Laing, I warn you it will go easier for you if you abandon these denials once and for all and admit to these crimes.'

Aunt Bee said nothing, just continued to glare at the Minister.

'Will you repent of your malefice and admit to the charms and spells you laid upon Patrick Morton, injuring him to the point of death?'

'Morton is mistaken. You are mistaken. I am no witch.'

Cowper tried a third time: 'It will go ill for you if you do not confess, Mistress Laing. We have Morton's evidence of your cursing him at the Smiddy, of your casting spells the following day, and we have the fact that the boy himself remains grievously ill. Confess now and I promise it will go lightly for you.'

'I am no witch. A lie will damn my soul, Minister. I am no witch.'

I could see the anger burning in Mr. Cowper's eyes. He turned abruptly to consult with the others, and for

several minutes, I could not hear clearly what was said. All the while, Aunt Bee sat quietly, but I could see her hands trembling and her eyes stared fearfully at the group of men, as they whispered in the dark.

Mr. Cowper turned back to address her once more. This time his voice was icily calm:

'Very well Mistress Laing, you shall be taken from this place to be watched and warded by the people of this town. The Witchpricker shall be sent for to further examine you. Believe me witch, you shall be held until you surely confess your foul deeds. Seize her!'

Three of the men moved forward and roughly manhandling Aunt Bee, bound and gagged her and brought her out from the Kirk. Mr. Cowper marched behind them, and the others began to leave the Kirk in ones and twos. I heard one say Aunt Bee would be held overnight in the thieves' hole.

I sat trembling and shaking, clinging to the tree branch. I could not get my legs to work, to climb down and race back home to Davey. What was I to tell him? What was to become of us now?

CHAPTER SIX

Old Tom took us in. Father had once saved Tom's life at sea and Tom had given his word to Aunt Bee that we should not be left without a home, should anything happen to her. After running home, I roused Davey and brought him with me to Tom's cottage.

Aunt Bee was held for five days and nights without sleep or food, watched over by the baillies of the town. The Witchpricker came and pricked her body countless times each day with a long brass needle, to test for the Devil's Mark, a sure sign of her being a witch. All those accused of witchcraft were routinely searched for the Devil's Mark. Any brown patch of skin or blemish of any kind would be considered as evidence of guilt. Men were employed as prickers. They would pierce such marks with a long pin. If the accused did not scream or the spot did not bleed they were considered to be guilty. Aunt Bee told us later that the Witchpricker pricked her shoulders, back and thighs so often that the blood gushed from her as he pressed the needle deeper and deeper into her.

All the time, she was being urged to confess. Mr. Cowper came and went constantly, not allowing her to sleep, commanding her to confess and promising that if she did so, the pricking would stop. Names were suggested to her of others in the town, also suspected of being witches. 'Name these, confess, and the pain will cease. Confess your own witchcraft, name the others, the pain will stop.' Aunt Bee endured this for six full days, without sleep nor rest of any sort. Finally, exhausted and confused, she did as they told her and confessed.

Prompted, she named several others in the town as being witches. She told us later that Mr Cowper recited off their names to her:

'Is Isabell Adam a witch?'

'Yes, yes,' muttered Aunt Bee wearily. 'Janet Cornfoot?'

In a whisper, 'Aye.'

'Nicolas Lawson and Thomas Brown?' 'Aye.'

'Janet Horsborough?'

'Aye.'

'Lillias Wallace?'

'Aye, let me be,' she pleaded.

These six were immediately seized and likewise subjected to witchpricking and other cruelties. Deprived of any sleep or comfort, they too in due course 'confessed their crimes'.

After this 'confession', Aunt Bee was finally allowed to sleep and eat. She quickly recovered her senses and realized the terrible wrong that had occurred. She cried out to her jailers that she that she had been forced to confess: 'they urged me continually to confess; and I said what they suggested to me, to be rid of the torture.' She was innocent, the others were innocent, her confession had been forced from her and a terrible injustice had been done. In

her anguish she would not be silenced and so Mr. Cowper was sent for. He was so enraged by this further denial that he had her placed in the stocks, her feet secured in the holes and chained in place for all to see as they passed by. There she remained for several days. Old Tom would not let us see her, for he was still terribly afraid that we too might be accused of malefice.

However, when we heard that Aunt Bee was to be cast into the dungeon, to be held there until her trial, we begged Tom to take us to her. We hardly recognized her - she was caked in mud and dried blood from her wounds and her clothes were torn and filthy. As they took her out of the stocks, the men again abused her, slapping her hard and punching her. Aunt Bee was beyond speaking any words to us, indeed I do not think she recognized us at all, so severe was her suffering. We came away very quietly after that, each holding one of Tom's hands, biting back our tears at what we had just witnessed. Aunt Bee was to remain in the dungeon for five full months, without heat or light, and with only scraps for food.

Davey and I continued to live with Old Tom. He made very sure that we kept out of harm's way. We had to stay around the cottage and kailyard, and were only allowed to stray as far as the adjoining field. We rarely went beyond these boundaries, as fear of witchcraft still stalked the village, and Tom lived in constant fear that we too would be accused.

Late one afternoon, Tom brought a stranger to visit with us. He was tall, a rich gentleman, with fine clothes and boots. He had brilliant blue eyes, the bluest eyes I have ever seen and a kind smile that lit up his entire face. I thought him quite old, as his hair was white and his face quite lined with wrinkles.

Tom brought him to where Davey and I were trouting in a small burn. Of course, Davey usually caught more in his boots than he did with his rod or net. More often than not, one or t'other of us ended up completely drookit from playing games or splashing each other, but once in a while, we would catch a tiddler or two which Tom would fry up for supper. It was a calm and peaceful place, so I was not alarmed when I looked up and saw them coming towards us.

'Isobel, David, this gentleman is a Mr. Laidlaw, come to Pittenweem all the way from St Andrews. He very much wants to meet you, as he has heard about your Aunt Bee

and all her troubles.'

Tom immediately saw me stiffen and Davey run at once to hide behind me - we were both terrified that this stranger wanted to do further harm to Aunt Bee or ourselves.

'Nae bairns, Mr. Laidlaw is a friend to us. He wants to help Beatrix and the others. He feels that a great wrong has been done here. Is that not so, sir?'

Mr. Laidlaw nodded to Tom and to us.

'Tom is right.' He smiled at us - 'Isobel and David, is it?'

Davey surprised me by speaking up – I was just getting ready to answer for us both. 'I'm Davey sir, and this is Iso. Leastways, that is what our Mother and Aunt Bee always called us,' piped up Davey, peeping out from behind me.

'Well Davey, my name is William. Do you know my name never gets shortened to anything at all?' He knelt beside Davey. 'If my big sister gets annoyed with me, she makes my name *longer* and calls me 'William John Laidlaw' in a very loud voice indeed. I have been known to jump a whole three feet in the air when my sister gets annoyed.'

Davey grinned and asked him:'And do you have any brothers, sir?'

'I do Davey. One brother, James, my younger brother. But he does not live with Margaret, that's my sister, and myself.'

'Is he married with boys and girls of his own, perhaps?' asked Davey.

'I don't think he is married yet, Davey, but he lives far away from us, right across the ocean, so he may be, for all I know.'

I had not said anything at this point, and Mr. Laidlaw

turned to me. 'James is partly why I am come to Pittenweem. I miss him very much, Isobel, as I am sure you would miss Davey if anything happened to him. You see, James left Scotland, many years ago. He left because he too was accused of witchcraft, just like your Aunt Beatrix.'

I gasped. Whatever I had been expecting him to say, it was not this!

'Let me tell you his story.' said Mr. Laidlaw.

CHAPTER SEVEN

Mr. Laidlaw sat down on the mossy grass in the open field, where he could see if anyone approached, and motioned for Davey, Tom and I to join him. He then began to tell us about James.

'Ever since James left Scotland, I have been keenly interested in stories like yours - people who have seen their families destroyed by accusations of witchcraft. You see, James was a Kirk Minister just like Mr. Cowper, yet even this did not protect him from such accusations.'

Neither Davey nor I could believe what Mr. Laidlaw was saying.

'Niver a minister?' said Davey.

'Yes Davey, he was a Minister but this did not save him. Some of the women in his town were talked about as being witches. One or two of these women were healers - they brewed herbs to help people when they were sick and one in particular was very gifted with animals. *This* woman had a falling out with one of the farmers and slowly stories about her started to circulate about the place. There had been real witches found in the next parish, you see, so it was easily believed by some that this woman too could be a witch. But my brother knew about the great argument that had occurred with the farmer, and so when some of his Elders came to him urging the case against these women, he resisted.'

'The Elders kept pressing him, but he remained firm. After some time, whispers started about James himself and it was put about that he too might be a witch. He knew if he remained he might be imprisoned, so the night he was supposed to be examined, he took his horse and rode like the wind to Margaret and me. We hid him for several days and then helped him get to England. From there, he managed to get on a ship across to New England, to a place called Williamsburg, in Virginia. That was many years ago, and we have not seen him since. But we do know he is alive and we are thankful to God for that.'

'When I came to St Andrews to visit with friends, I heard of all that had been happening here. So I have come to see if Beatrix Laing is truly a witch or just a poor woman caught up in malicious story telling.'

'Like James,' I said. It was the first time I had spoken since he arrived.

He smiled at me, 'Yes Iso, just like my poor James. I have heard tell that the poor demented laddie Morton started all this, but his wits are now so addled by his illness, it is impossible to be sure of the truth of anything he says.'

'Mr. Cowper believes him though sir. He and Patrick truly believe that Aunt Bee is a witch, which is why she has been imprisoned all this time,' I said.

'But you Isobel, what do you believe? Tell me.'

'I never saw her do any witchcraft sir, and I have known her all my life. 'Tis true she had a gift with herbs and cures, but she never used that to harm anyone.' I paused, and asked him the question I had longed to ask someone since this whole thing started:

'I don't think Aunt Bee is a witch, Sir. But why would Patrick Morton say so? To meddle with witchcraft is sic a terrible thing, why say it if it were not so?'

'I don't know, Iso. I can tell you what I think may have happened. Sometimes lads and lassies want to be important. They want people to pay attention to them, to notice them. Maybe Patrick was a little like that? After all, we can all feel a little like that sometimes. Yet I also hear from some of the people here that Patrick knew a lot about other cases of witchcraft that have happened. Some are even saying that Mr. Cowper told him about other parishes where real witches have been caught and punished.' I nodded at this point, because Davey and I had heard that too, in the early days, before Aunt Bee was imprisoned.

'So, maybe Patrick was thinking a lot about witchcraft and malefice even before he became ill. Maybe dwelling on it so much caused his illness. And in that illness, he accused Beatrix Laing of being a witch. I think there was no witchcraft here Iso, just a poor laddie deluded in his wits.'

'But they confessed, even Aunt Bee confessed! Why would they do sic a thing if it were not so?'

'Until she was examined, your Aunt denied everything, is that not so?

'Oh yes, sir, and we heard her deny it too, the day Mr. Kincaid and Mr. Bruce came to command her to attend the Session.' (And at the Session itself, I thought, but it was many months before I told Mr. Laidlaw of my secret visit to the Kirk the night of Aunt Bee's arrest).

'And remember Iso, she was pricked constantly, kept without food or light or sleep, for day after day. I cannot think how hard that must be. Maybe she would say anything to have that torment stop?   Because as soon as she was left alone and had a chance to regain her senses, she told how she had been forced to confess.'

'Yes sir, and it was then that they placed her in the stocks to punish her, and then they threw her in prison, and we have not seen her since,' I said and Davey began to greet quietly.

'It has been very hard for you, I know,' said Mr. Laidlaw in a very quiet voice. 'That is why I am here and why I wanted to see you. I hope to see Beatrix Laing very soon, and I hope to speak to her and hear her story and to

tell that to important people who may be able to help. I
wanted to meet you and to let you know that there is still
a little hope left.'

Mr. Laidlaw came to see us regularly after that. He
went to Mr. Cowper and the burgesses and angrily protested
the treatment of Aunt Bee and the others. He wrote many
letters and wrote a pamphlet for all to read, decrying the
treatment of those accused. After many weeks, he managed
to get in to see Aunt Bee, by bribing one of the guards - no
official access was ever granted to him. He found her in
a miserable state, but she was able to tell her story to him.
et the Kirk Session would not budge. They maintained that
the witches were guilty as charged. We do not know to
whom Mr. Laidlaw spoke, nor how much work he did,
nor if he worked alone, but in August 1704, five months
after her imprisonment, Aunt Bee and the others were freed
by the Sheriff of Fife, the Earl of Rothes, for lack of evidence.
Aunt Bee, seemingly doomed to be burnt at the stake as a
witch, was free at last.

CHAPTER EIGHT

Aunt Bee seemed much older and frailer when she came home. She clung to us and held us very tightly, saying our names over and over again to herself. She had no energy or strength, so Davey and I did much of the work around the cottage and garden, with Tom's help. One or two people came to visit, but mostly folk stayed away. At night, laddies would throw stones at our cottage and the three of us would huddle indoors, too afraid to say anything or to chase them, for fear of what they might do to us. Aunt Bee began to make plans to leave Pittenweem and move along the coast to Crail or St Andrews. Over the months, her strength slowly began to return and she resolved that we move and try and find work elsewhere once summer came. However, in January 1705, a terrible event occurred, which hastened our departure. I was in the cottage, alone, when Tom came rushing up:

'Iso, the crowd is behind me; you and Davey must run and hide.'

I stood looking at him - what did he mean 'run and hide?'

'Now, lass!' he bellowed at me. 'The crowd will be here any minute. Where's Davey?'

'He's out the back, I'll fetch him in.'

'Nay lass, go, get him and go away and hide.'

'But Tom...'

He hustled me out the door.

'There's talk Janet Cornfoot is back. Folk are mad to find her and there's talk about a lynching here tonight. I met Beatrix on the road, she has fled already. You and Davey are not safe, I'll come find you when it's all over. Go lass, go!'

So I ran. I found Davey by our burn, and taking him by the hand I ran as fast as I could. All the time, my mind was racing - where would we be safe, where could we hide? It was a bitter cold January day and the sky was already darkening, when I heard angry voices behind me, dozens of them, growing louder by the second. Where could I hide?

I was not far from the Kirk. Panicking, I remembered the tree and grabbing Davey pulled him over to it. We climbed up as fast as we could go, our legs trembling. With no leaves to hide us, I prayed that with twilight falling we would not be seen. Moments later, the crowd started milling over the grass in front of the Kirk. There were maybe forty or fifty people, men and women, shouting angrily.

'The witch will no' be here, by the Kirk. She'd be afeart to be this close to a Kirk.'

'Aye, richt enough.'

At this a murmur of agreement ran around the crowd. We heard them discuss where Janet would likely be hidden:

'Could be she's headed back down to the shore?

'She'll be lyin' low in some byre somewhere, amongst the other animals.'

Then a cry went up: 'They've got her! Skulking out back of the Horsborough place. They're taking her down to the harbour!'

The crowd turned down past the Kirk and on towards the harbour. Davey and I stayed perfectly still for a long time, hardly daring to breathe. When we were absolutely sure there was no one left behind, when all we could hear was the sound of our own hearts pounding, we slipped down the tree and ran to Old Tom's place, as silently as we could. We went into the cottage and hid in the far corner, pulling an old blanket tight over our heads, so no one would see us if they looked in. Tom found us there much later, still huddled together in fright.

Janet Cornfoot was seized by the crowd and dragged screaming down to the shore line, where she was tied to a rope 'twixt ship and shore until nearly drowned, pelted with rocks and abused by the crowd. Finally, she was brought on shore again and, almost unconscious, laid down with a heavy door placed over her. Onto this door the mob, taking turns and laughing, placed heavy rocks and boulders. To make absolutely sure that the poor woman was dead, someone brought a horse and sleigh, and rode back and forth across the door until all life was extinguished. The date was January 30, in the year of our Lord, 1705.

That night Aunt Bee fled Pittenweem forever. When Tom found us at his cottage, he told us they had arranged that she would send for us as soon as she was safe. We were to tell no one of her destination - St Andrews. Terrified that something would happen to us, Tom would not let us leave the cottage. We lived like this until one

44

week after the murder, when Mr. Laidlaw arrived, with news of Aunt Bee. She was safe in St Andrews, but was too unwell to look after us. Nor could we stay in Pittenweem after all that had happened; the risk not just to ourselves, but to Tom for standing by us, was too great. Mr. Laidlaw had asked Aunt Bee to allow him to take us to stay with him until she was well enough to care for us again. She had agreed.

On our last day in Pittenweem, Mr. Laidlaw took us back to Aunt Bee's abandoned cottage to pick up our few belongings, and had them carried down to the harbour where we were to sail on the high tide. Usually, I loved the chance to go on a boat, to feel the water beneath me and taste the tang of salt in the air. But that February day, it was rough weather, with a strong wind blowing and I do not think I have ever been so cold in my life. My very breath seemed to freeze in the icy air and my eyes were wet with tears from the biting wind. I listened to the groaning of the ropes as the sails caught the wind. My heart was cold and empty as I watched our harbour grow smaller, and smaller, and we left Pittenweem behind forever.

CHAPTER NINE

Two people died in Pittenweem during those terrible times: Janet Cornfoot, whose death I have written about here, and Thomas Brown, who starved to death while held awaiting trial. Aunt Bee fled to St Andrews, and lives there still. She is not well, and we are ever anxious about her health. Her ordeal meant her body and spirit were broken and she may never fully recover. We pray for her every day. The other witches were also freed, on bail or with a fine. Some fled the town, some live there still. A full enquiry was organized into the lynching of Janet Corn foot, but we do not know if anyone will be brought to trial for her murder.

Davey and I have a home with the Laidlaws for as long as we wish. We have been told this many times. Sometimes, when I sit and read the Psalms with Mr. Laidlaw, I see his eyes fill with tears. Sometimes too I catch him looking at me or Davey with a face so still and sad that it would break my heart, if it were not already broken in so many pieces.

Miss Laidlaw is as fussy as ever yet she has grown fond of us, especially Davey. When Davey is tired or ill he calls her 'My Maggie'. I do believe he would just as soon have Miss Laidlaw sit by his side and comfort him as myself.

It has grown late in the afternoon and the shadows are beginning to lengthen. I am sitting high in my tree listening to the birds calling to one another as they swoop to and fro. Far down below I see Davey wandering aimlessly in our little vegetable patch, brushing some of the plants with a broken twig dangling from his fingers. Miss Laidlaw is watching him from the kitchen door. It is very quiet and peaceful here in my tree, with just the crows cawing and the leaves rustling in the breeze. I wonder if Mr. Laidlaw will like what I have written? I close my braw blue journal and put my things in my pocket, making ready for my climb down. I hear a murmur of voices, two men talking quietly on the brae next to the house. The next moment Mr. Laidlaw calls out:

'Maggie, Iso, Davey, I'm home.'

I see him stride into the garden and I realize I am smiling as I look down at him. He looks tired from his journey, but is full of smiles as Davey runs to him. He catches him and tosses him high in the air. I must show him my journal and all I have written! I make ready toscramble down, but then I change my mind and stop. I

look back up at the golden rose speckled sky and stretch out my fingers high above my head. I can feel the leaves dance lightly on my finger tips as they push higher and higher through the rich green canopy. I close my eyes and reach out to touch the sky:

'Thank God for Mother and Father. And God Bless Aunt Bee and Tom and keep them safe.'

Then I call out to my family below and scramble down to welcome Mr. Laidlaw home.

Patrick Morton later withdrew his tale of witchcraft and malefice.

He had fabricated the entire story.

GLOSSARY

PSALMS One of the most popular books of the Old Testament in the Christian Bible.Ê There are 150 Psalms (songs or poems) in total.

KIRK SESSION The governing body of a local congregation of the Church of Scotland, made up of Kirk Elders. In 1704, these would all be men, of some standing or importance in their community.

KIRK ELDER A member of the Kirk Session

PARISH The local geographical area in which the church operates.

PANTILES A curved roof tile, commonly found in Fife coastal villages in the 1700s and still seen today.

BAILIE A magistrate or law officer.

BURGESS A member of the governing body of a town.

SHERIFF The chief Judge or law officer in an area.

MALEFICE Harmful magic; charming with evil intent; Witchcraft.

WITCHPRICKER Hired by local townspeople to scrutinize and examine suspected witches. Witchprickers were paid by results, and the methods they used invariably involved both physical and psychological torture.

STOCKS An instrument of public punishment in which the prisoner is placed, with feet secured through two holes in a wooden frame. Prisoners would then be displayed to the local community and be insulted by passers by.

KAILYARD Cabbage patch; vegetable patch.

READERS' NOTES

In the sixteenth century, belief in witchcraft, fairies and spirits was commonplace, and deeply ingrained across all social classes in Scotland. The *1563 Witchcraft Act* interpreted all acts of magic, charming or witchcraft as a threat to the established order, punishable by the most severe penalties.

From 1590 through to the repeal of the Act in 1736, there were many cases of local and national witchcraft hunts in both Scotland and England. These took place against the background of both the *Reformation* and later the *Restoration*, when the need to maintain social control and good order was a key aim for all the governing interests of the land.

During this era, thousands of people were accused and found guilty of witchcraft.

People believed that witches had unusual powers – the ability to charm and heal, to harm and curse. Those accused of witchcraft were independent women (and occasionally men), generally unmarried or widowed, possibly estranged from their families. Some were midwives and healers in their communities. They may have had personal characteristics which were regarded as anti- social. Unhappily it was then all too easy for them to become *scapegoats* for their communities.

Symptoms of *sleep deprivation* include hallucination, paranoia and disorientation. Modern practitioners of sleep deprivation during interrogation of prisoners are alleged to have included the KGB (former USSR), the Japanese and others during WWII, the British Army against the IRA in the early 1970s, the Apartheid regime in South Africa, as well as contemporary Israel, China, Saudi Arabia and Iran. It is believed to be currently used by US forces at Guantanomo Bay, Cuba.

Loss of sleep is intensely stressful, resulting in the loss of the ability to think and act coherently. The desire to sleep becomes paramount, and one will give almost anything to be permitted to do so. After two nights, hallucinations can begin, after three or more various forms of psychosis can set in. Those who have endured sleep deprivation comment that the desire to sleep becomes more dominant than the desire to eat or drink.

We are horrified by the events in Pittenweem in this story, especially as they are based on true events. Thank goodness we didn't live in the eighteenth century, we may tell ourselves. Yet even today, torture and punishment of suspects is commonplace in many countries throughout the world, as monitored by organisations such as Amnesty International, and the Medical Foundation for the Care of Victims of Torture.

Teachers reading this may wish to note that this book dovetails with the Scottish curriculum in

- Environmental Studies
- Personal and Social Health Education
- Philosophy
- Language

Further information on Rooshie-Doo books, and suggestions for their use in schools, can be found on the publisher's website at www.galluspublications.com

If you have enjoyed this book, you may also enjoy…

Reformed! A story of Jenny Geddes by Helen Welsh

Murderers! A story of Burke and Hare by Karen Doherty

Threat! A story of Mary Slessor by Karen Doherty

Cannibals! A story of Sawney Bean by Helen Welsh